Pip Gets Wheels!

by Natalie Jane Parker

A BROLLY BOOK

Blip and Pip were the best of friends, and they enjoyed each other's company.

Blip would often sit with Pip, and tell him about his adventures in the forest.

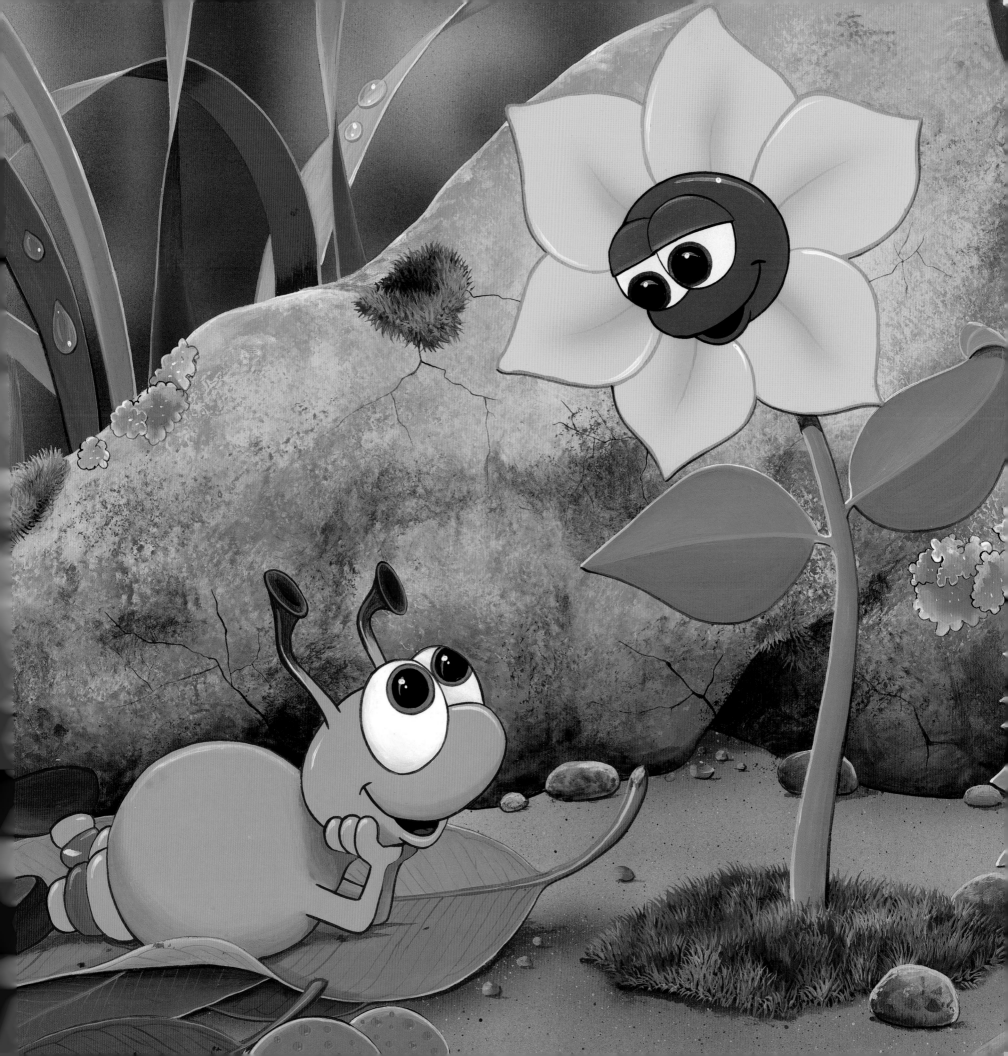

"A few nights ago, it was very hot so I went for a long walk," Blip told Pip.

"The stars were very bright, and they seemed to be bobbing around in the sky. Then I realised they weren't stars at all. They were fire flies!"

"The next day, the creek near my home was very smooth. I walked up to the edge and gazed into the cool, still water.

"To my surprise, I saw my own face smiling back at me!"

"Then, just yesterday, I stumbled upon a big pile of toadstools. They were spongy and soft, so I climbed on top and bounced up and down. It was great fun!"

At last, Blip finished telling Pip his stories. It was then he noticed Pip was looking very sad.

"What's wrong?" he asked.

"I'm tired of standing still!" cried Pip. "I want to come with you and visit these wonderful places you tell me about! But how can I? I'm rooted to one spot!"

Blip tried to comfort his friend, but it was no use.

"What can we do?" they wondered.

"Try putting him in a cart and taking him with you!" they heard a voice say. A nearby ladybug had overheard their whole conversation.

"How, Miss?" they asked.

"Miss? I'm no miss!" replied the ladybug. "My name is Bob. Let me ask my family for help."

Bob flew off and soon returned with his family. Blip and Pip were amazed to see how many ladybugs he had with him.

The ladybugs had brought lots of pieces of wood with them. Together with Blip and Pip, they worked out a way to build the cart.

"I have some wheels and rope at home that we can use!" shouted Blip, rushing off to fetch them. When he returned, he and the ladybugs worked all afternoon to build Pip's cart.

At last they were finished. They filled the cart with good rich soil then dug around Pip to uproot him from the ground. Then they gently lifted him up and placed him in the cart.

"This is really comfy!" said Pip. His new friends gave him a drink of water and he wriggled his roots and settled in.

"Now," asked Blip, "where would you like to go first?"